GW00731340

Also by John Foley

Seven Simple and Slightly Silly Stories

***Another* Seven Simple and Slightly Silly Stories**

The Bear in the Fifth Floor Flat

plus

Once Bitten, Twice...

—

John Foley

Illustrations by Alice Hawthorn

First published in 2019 by QuizzicalWorks

www.quizzicalworks.com
email: quizzicalworks@gmail.com
Facebook: johnrfoley123
Twitter: @quizzicalworks
Instagram: @quizzical.works

www.dogsdogscatsdogs.com
email: alice@dogsdogscatsdogs.com
Instagram: @dogsdogscatsdogs

ISBN: 978-1-9997437-6-5

Creative and Print by SpiffingCovers

For

Registered charity number 222377

Contents

Part One:
Scruffy, and how it all started

This is the story of a little girl and a very special bear who lived together on the fifth floor of a block of flats in south London. The girl's name is Ruthie, and the bear's name… well, you don't need to know his name right now as that comes later. First, as with almost every story, it's a good idea to begin at the beginning. So…

It all started when Ruthie was five and a half years old. At that time she and her parents lived in a handsome house on the edge of Hampstead Heath. The house was a big house on three floors, a higgledy-piggledy house full of nooks and crannies and interesting places to hide. And always, or so it seemed, there was fun and laughter.

Ruthie, in particular, was very happy. If she wasn't laughing she was smiling, sometimes with a smile as wide as a dinner plate. She had bright, curly red hair (which she liked), and on her nose and cheeks a sprinkling of freckles (which she didn't).

She had a dog which wasn't quite a poodle and wasn't quite a spaniel. Ruthie and her mother had found him on the Heath one spring day. Ruthie, who was very friendly, made the mistake of talking to the dog and stroking him and throwing a stick again and again – and for the dog that was it. As far as he was concerned he'd found a wonderful playmate and he wasn't going to let her out of his sight.

Of course this caused a bit of a problem when it was time to go home.

'Don't encourage him,' said Ruthie's mother. 'Just keep walking.'

So they kept walking – off the Heath and down the quiet road that led to their house. But the dog kept walking too, trotting along closely beside Ruthie with his tail wagging as though he and his new best friend had belonged to each other for years.

At one point halfway down the road Ruthie's mother stopped and spoke firmly to the dog. 'It's time you went home now,' she said, and the dog cocked his head to one side and woofed softly, as if in agreement.

And then to their surprise the dog sat down.

'Now's our chance,' Ruthie's mother whispered. 'Just walk away, and whatever you do don't turn round.'

Ruthie didn't like this instruction, but she did as she was told and walked away with her mother. But then as they reached the gate to the small garden in front of their house, she felt she just had to turn and look one last time. The dog was still waiting on the pavement, sitting where they had left him, but as soon as he saw Ruthie looking back at him he barked joyously and lolloped up to her.

'Oh, Ruthie,' said her mother, rather crossly. 'Well, he's not coming in the house.'

'Can he just–?' began Ruthie. But her mother said 'no' very firmly. Then leaving the dog outside the gate she led Ruthie up the short path, opened the front door to let her in first, followed behind her, and shut the door.

And that was that. Or so she thought.

Ruthie was very quiet for the rest of the afternoon. She was still quiet when her father arrived home from work that evening. When he remarked on this quietness Ruthie's mother told him all about the dog on the Heath and how it had followed them home.

'Is that the dog sitting outside the gate?' he asked.

'He's still there?' asked Ruthie. 'Can I go and see him? Can I? Just for a minute?'

'No,' said her mother. 'Time you were in bed. Go on now.'

Ruthie opened her mouth to complain, but before she could say anything her father surprised them both. 'Perhaps we could get a dog one day,' he said. 'After all, we do live in the perfect place for one.'

'Oh, yes yes yes!' cried Ruthie.

'And who's going to look after it?' her mother asked. 'Feed it and take it for walks and do all the other things you have to do with dogs?'

'Me!' said Ruthie. 'I can do it all.'

'I'm sure you can,' said her father, laughing.

'Well... perhaps for your birthday,' said her mother, and her father agreed, 'Yes, perhaps for your birthday.'

And that, for the moment, was that.

After breakfast the next morning Ruthie's father left for work at the usual time. A few minutes later he was back in the kitchen again. 'That dog's still there,' he said.

'It's not coming in the house!' said Ruthie's mother. And Ruthie's father sighed and went off to work, and Ruthie went upstairs to play in her room and peep through the curtains at the dog sitting outside by the front gate, waiting patiently.

The dog was still there that afternoon when Ruthie and her mother went back to the Heath, and of course he went with them too, and for the next hour or so Ruthie threw sticks and the dog chased them and brought them back, and when they both tired of that game they chased each other. Round and round the trees they went, faster and faster, until in the end they could run no more and they collapsed in a happy heap on the grass.

When it was time to go home, the dog trotted alongside Ruthie and her mother, looking up at his new best friend and wagging his tail just as he had done the day before. But this time her mother didn't say 'no'. Instead, she opened the front gate wide for Ruthie and the dog to pass through, and together they walked up the path, and Ruthie looked at her mother and her mother smiled back. Then she unlocked the door and the three of them went inside together. And when Ruthie's father returned that night he didn't say 'no' and he didn't say 'yes' either, but just patted the dog and said what a fine fellow he was, and life in the

house continued as though the dog had always been there.

To begin with, Ruthie and her mother and her father called the dog just 'Dog'. But at breakfast one morning two or three days later her father said, 'Dog needs a name'. And he turned to Ruthie and asked, 'What do you think?'

Ruthie had already thought. 'Scruffy. His name's Scruffy,' she said immediately. Scruffy obviously thought it a good name for he woofed twice and thumped his tail on the kitchen floor.

When the weekend came and Scruffy still showed no signs of wanting to leave, Ruthie's father insisted on taking him first to the police station and then to the vet.

'But why?' asked Ruthie.

'Because someone must have lost him, and they'll want him back again,' said her father.

This was not good news for Ruthie.

At the police station the sergeant at the desk looked at Scruffy and smiled and called him 'a very handsome chappie'. He also said that no one had yet reported a dog like him to be missing, but that he'd make a note of it. After that, Ruthie and her father and Scruffy continued on down the hill to the vet's surgery. The vet examined the dog and was pleased to say that he was young and healthy, but as there was no collar or microchip to identify him, and as no one had phoned or emailed about a missing dog like Scruffy there was no way of knowing to whom he belonged.

Then the vet suggested putting up some notices. 'To see if anyone claims him,' he said.

'And what will happen if nobody wants him?' Ruthie asked, hoping desperately that the vet would say the words she wanted to hear.

'Well...,' said the vet, and looked at her father. And after a pause her father replied: 'If nobody claims him then I suppose we'd better look after him.'

This of course was just the news Ruthie had been hoping for. She jumped up and down and clapped her hands, and seeing her happiness Scruffy woofed and wagged his tail even harder.

On the way home her father had a note of warning. 'Listen, Ruthie, if we keep Scruffy he's your responsibility. You must look after him. Not your mother, and not me, but you. Is that clear?'

'My responsibility, yes,' she agreed.

That afternoon Ruthie's father took a photo of Scruffy on his phone and transferred it to his computer. Underneath the photo, which showed Scruffy with his head to one side and his pink tongue hanging out, he wrote a description of the dog, where he'd been found and how to claim him back. After this, her father printed a dozen posters and Ruthie took them to the kitchen table and coloured them with crayons, and the next day she and her mother and Scruffy walked round the neighbourhood and stuck the posters with sticky tape or tied them with string to trees and fences. And at each and every place Ruthie said to herself, 'I do hope no one reads this.'

LOST DOG
AND
FOUND
NOT QUITE A POODLE
AND NOT QUITE A SPANIEL
FOUND ON HAMPSTEAD HEATH
IF THIS DOG BELONGS TO YOU CALL
07973 117889

A week went by and no one rang her father's mobile to ask about the dog. A few days after that there was a heavy rainstorm and the next morning the posters were all smudged and unreadable.

'Well, that's that,' Ruthie told Scruffy, and they were both very happy.

By now Scruffy was part of the family. He wasn't a very smart dog (or so Ruthie's father said), but he knew the rules: exactly what he was allowed to do and what he wasn't, where he was allowed to go and where he wasn't, and for the most part he stuck to those rules. Occasionally there were slip-ups, usually to do with chewing something that didn't agree with him, or sleeping somewhere he shouldn't have slept, but Ruthie kept him out of trouble as much as possible.

Of course, on good weather days there was the Heath, where there were squirrels to chase and sometimes even rabbits. Scruffy never caught one, and even if he had caught one he probably wouldn't have known what to do next. But that was not the point. For him the game was running and chasing. There was running and chasing on bad weather days, too, especially in the long hall downstairs with its polished tiles, or on the landing upstairs with its polished wood, and often when Scruffy raced up and down the hall or the landing too quickly he found he couldn't stop in time before he skidded into the wall at the other end. Then he would shake the bump from his head and sit for a moment looking rather surprised, but as soon as he recovered he would woof 'oooh, that was fun' and do exactly the same again.

The house near the Heath was a big house with a big garden at the back, and sometimes there was a gardener to help Ruthie's father grow flowers and vegetables. To help Ruthie's mother there was Marta who cleaned and occasionally looked after Ruthie and would speak in a strange voice using words she didn't understand, and sometimes when Ruthie's mother was not hard at work in her study doing whatever she did she would make cakes and biscuits which they would all enjoy at teatime around the kitchen table or, when the weather was fine, in the garden.

That first year with Scruffy was a very happy year. And then one day it all began to change, and although Ruthie's parents loved each other dearly, in the second year they started to fight. Ruthie didn't know what the fighting was about, but once it began they fought more and more – arguing and shouting at each other and sometimes breaking cups and plates, and even on one very noisy occasion a large mirror. And then there were tears and more shouting and slamming of doors.

After some months of this fighting Ruthie's mother and father were both very unhappy. So, too, was Ruthie; so, too, was Scruffy. And so, too, was the higgledy-piggledy house, and the fun and laughter and running and chasing and games of hide-and-seek in the nooks and crannies were no more.

And then suddenly one day, Ruthie's father was there no more either. He had gone away.

No one knew where he had gone, but the small black briefcase he usually took to work in the City every weekday morning was gone, and the big brown suitcase he always took on holiday was also gone. When Ruthie first asked where her father was, her mother looked solemnly at her. She put her hand to her mouth and shook her head, and for a moment it seemed as though she was going to cry, but then she took Ruthie's hand, stroked it and said quietly, 'I don't know.' She said the same a few days later when Ruthie asked again, and the same two days after that: 'I don't know.'

And then one morning more than a week later the postman brought a letter. Ruthie thought it must be from her father because it had his special handwriting in blue ink. And yet there was something about the writing on the envelope that was not quite the same. Gone were the twirls and twiddles and big letters that Ruthie loved; now instead the letters were smaller, neater, colder.

Ruthie sat patiently as her mother opened the letter and began to read.

'Is it from Daddy?' she asked at last, and her mother nodded. For a while there was more silence. Her mother read through the letter once, and then again, and then a third time. Finally, she said to Ruthie: 'Daddy's gone to find himself.'

To find himself? Ruthie didn't understand this at all. She knew all about finding things. For example, if she lost a sock or a doll or a crayon she would look for it, and eventually she would find it because it was nearly always under the bed or on the kitchen table or in the little pink satchel with all the rest of her school bits and bobs. But surely, she thought, before you can find things you need to lose them. And how can you lose *yourself*?

'But Daddy's not lost, is he?' she asked.

Her mother smiled and stroked Ruthie's hair. 'Well...,' she said, 'sometimes when a person doesn't know who he is–'

Ruthie looked puzzled. 'That's silly! Daddy knows who he is!'

'Well, yes,' said her mother. She tried again. 'Sometimes when a person isn't very happy with his life... with the way things are going, he needs to go away for a few days, to think about–'

'A few days!' cried Ruthie. By now her father had been gone more than ten days.

*

Summer came and went. From time to time a letter arrived from Ruthie's father to her mother, and once or twice there was a short letter for Ruthie herself. And then one afternoon, just as the leaves were falling from the trees and Ruthie was beginning to get used to her father's empty place at the table, something dreadful happened.

Ruthie and her mother and Scruffy were walking home from their games on the Heath. As they approached the house Ruthie saw a squirrel sitting on the wall by their front gate. Scruffy saw it too, and

giving a joyful bark as if to say 'oh, what fun!' he bounded up to the wall. The squirrel looked down at Scruffy, then turning his back, he shook his bushy tail as if to say 'come on, silly dog, catch me if you can!' The next moment he leapt down onto the pavement and darted round the corner and along the quiet little street into the busy main road beyond. Of course, this was too tempting for Scruffy, and before Ruthie and her mother could stop him he was racing after the squirrel onto the busy road where just at that moment a red double-decker bus was rushing by far too fast to stop in time.

Afterwards, Ruthie remembered only three sounds: the sudden screech of brakes, a dull thud, a short, sharp yelp of pain. And then silence. By the time Ruthie and her mother reached the scene the bus driver was out of his seat and standing over the crumpled heap in the road and shaking his head. 'I never had a chance!' he said crossly, and then as if to blame anyone who was listening he complained: 'He should have been on a lead.'

'Don't look,' said her mother and tried to shield her daughter's eyes.

But Ruthie looked and she saw. And she dropped to her knees and cradled Scruffy's head in her lap, and as the light in his eyes dimmed and died she wept.

A few days later, Ruthie's mother said, 'Now that Scruffy...' She hesitated a moment, then started again. 'Now that Scruffy has gone...' she said, then stopped altogether as she saw the tears pricking Ruthie's eyes. And she lifted Ruthie onto her lap and held her tight and stroked her hair. After a while she spoke again.

'Do you remember Uncle Ted?' she asked brightly.

Ruthie looked up at her mother, her eyes now red with tears. 'Of course,' she answered. After all, how could she forget Uncle Ted, especially as she liked him so much, even though he was rather odd?

Uncle Ted was her mother's brother. Although a few years older than her, he looked much younger, almost boyish. This was partly because of the large, round, black-rimmed spectacles he wore. They made his eyes seem much bigger than they really were and gave him the appearance of a startled owl.

He was an artist, and spent his days and sometimes his nights drawing cartoons for newspapers and magazines, and whenever he came to tea he would bring Ruthie drawing paper and coloured pencils. Sometimes he would show her his latest drawings, and while some of them were funny, there were others, serious ones with cross-looking men and women shouting and shaking their fists in the air, that she didn't understand at all.

Most of all, Ruthie remembered Uncle Ted's bald head and the striped and floppy woollen hat he liked to wear even in summer.

'No hats at the table,' her mother would say each time he came to tea. And Uncle Ted would make a face and take off the woolly hat and put it in his pocket, but as soon as tea was over and he was ready to leave he would take out the hat and pull it back on his head.

'He says we can live with him for a while,' her mother continued.

'But we live here,' said Ruthie.

'I know, darling. I know,' said her mother. 'But...' And now it was time for her mother's eyes to redden with tears. Finally, she drew a deep breath and spoke again: 'I think we're going to have to let the house.'

Ruthie was puzzled and she immediately forgot about Uncle Ted and his bald head and woolly hat.

'Let the house do what?' she asked.

'No,' said her mother. She started to say something about no money and problems with the bank, then stopped and said instead, 'It's too big for just the two of us, so some other people will come and live here, and in the meantime we'll go to live with Uncle Ted. Just until Daddy comes back.'

'And when will that be?'

'Soon, I hope,' said her mother. 'Very soon.'

What happened after that seemed to happen very quickly so that there was no time to be sad or unhappy or even to think about what was going on, as Ruthie and her mother cleaned and tidied the house and filled some large boxes with valuables and some other boxes with clothes and even Ruthie's toys and locked them away down in the cellar. The following afternoon a woman in a smart blue suit came to inspect the house and the garden and to measure all the rooms and to take some photographs. Just a few days after that a young man and woman came and muttered to each other in a foreign language and signed a piece of paper.

A week later, Ruthie and her mother moved out of the house near the Heath and went to live with Uncle Ted.

Part Two:
Measly, and how it all ended

Uncle Ted lived in Fountain House, a block of flats in a very different part of London on the other side of the river. Ruthie and her mother had taken a taxi laden with suitcases and a big cardboard box from their home in north London. As they crossed London Bridge Ruthie realised that it was the first time she had ever seen the river, let alone been south of it.

Half an hour later they approached Fountain House, and Ruthie said out loud, 'Where's the fountain?' and then quietly to herself, 'I don't think I'm going to like it here.'

As if in answer to her thought her mother said, 'We must make the best of it,' and then, 'I'm sure it won't be too bad.'

And surprisingly, as it turned out, it wasn't.

Although the building looked shabby and rather ugly and squashed on the outside as though someone very heavy had sat on it, on the inside – in the hall at least – it was really quite clean. There was a dark red carpet and on the wall a shiny panel of buttons with all the flats numbered. Ruthie's mother let Ruthie press the button for 53 and after a short while there was a crackle and they heard Uncle Ted's cheery voice: 'Hello, hello! Take the lift to the fifth floor and

I'll meet you at the door.'

And true to his word when the lift door opened on the fifth floor Uncle Ted was there to greet them with a big cheery grin. He had been away, working abroad somewhere for more than a year, and Ruthie hadn't seen him since he came back, but with his owlish eyes and his striped woolly hat he was just as she remembered him.

'Welcome! Welcome!' he said brightly, and he kissed Ruthie's mother and Ruthie. Then, picking up the box and her mother's suitcase (Ruthie insisted on carrying her own), he led them down a dimly-lit corridor smelling of cabbage and onions to a dark red door. To the right of the door was the number 53 in thick black paint.

'Just in time for tea,' he said, as he opened the door and took them into the hall. 'But first let me show you where you're sleeping. Jenny, you're in here,' he said, showing Ruthie's mother into a small room with a narrow bed in it. 'And you, Ruthie, in here.' And he showed her into an even smaller, narrower room next to her mother's.

'Normally this is my study–'

'But where will you work?' Ruthie's mother asked.

'At the kitchen table or at my little studio down the road. That's all I need really. And look, Ruthie, there's lots of paper and pencils inside this cupboard. There are paints as well, and you can use them as much as you like–'

'As long as you put the tops back on,' said her mother.

5
MAX LOAD 750KG
OR 10 PERSONS
NO SMOKING
5
4
3
2
1
G

'Very sensible!' said her uncle.

'But there isn't a bed,' said Ruthie.

'You're absolutely right! No room for one. So I got you a puff-puff bed.'

'What's a puff-puff bed?' Ruthie asked.

'Top marks for a very good question,' he replied, and from the cupboard he pulled out a large piece of what looked like a red canvas bag. 'Now you see this tube here?' (Ruthie nodded) 'Well, into this you blow and blow and you puff and puff, and after a whole heap of blowing and puffing you have your bed. And you know what?' (Ruthie shook her head) 'it's really quite comfortable. But plenty of time for that later. Right now I've something else to show you!'

And taking Ruthie by the hand he led her into a small kitchen.

'See what arrived just this morning,' said her uncle, pointing to the table and a package about twice the size of a shoe box, wrapped in brown paper. 'Someone's got a present. At least, I think it's a present.' He picked up the box and handed it to Ruthie. 'Now whose name is that?' he asked, tapping the address label.

'Mine!' shouted Ruthie, and then again as she recognised the handwriting, 'it's from Daddy!'

'I thought as much,' said Uncle Ted. 'The question is, do you open your present now, and then have tea, or have tea first and–'

'No!' squealed Ruthie. She was about to tear open the brown paper wrapping when she noticed the colourful stamp.

'What's E–I–R–E?' she asked, pointing to the name on the stamp.

'It's a country across the sea,' said her mother. 'Not far from here. And look, the postmark: Dublin. That's a big city where he posted it. Your father lived there a long time ago, before we met each other. We went there on our honeymoon.'

'So you did!' said Uncle Ted.

'What's a honey… honeymoon?' asked Ruthie.

'It's a time when...' Her mother paused, and for the first time in weeks she smiled. 'A time when we were very happy.'

For a moment there was a silence in the kitchen, then Uncle Ted said, 'Well now, enough of that! Aren't you going to open it?'

This was just the signal Ruthie had been waiting for, and she pulled away the sticky tape and tore off the brown paper till she uncovered a rather battered cardboard box. She hesitated a moment, looked up at her mother, and then down at the box. Finally she pulled open the lid and there inside, cushioned in old newspaper, lay a rather dirty-looking cream-coloured teddy bear covered from head to toe in what could have been red splodges but in some places looked more like red lips. Small but rather clumsily drawn lipstick-red lips.

'What on earth?' said her mother.

'I think they're supposed to be kisses,' said her uncle.

Ruthie's mother was about to say what a very odd present or some such thing, but Uncle Ted interrupted her: 'Look, Ruthie. There's this, too,' he said, and handed her a letter.

Ruthie wanted to hold the bear so she gave the letter to her mother to read aloud.

'My darling Ruthie,' her mother read: 'The other day I was walking down the street when I passed a very strange shop and I knew I had to go in. Inside, there was an old woman, a very old woman. I think she might have been a witch–'

'A witch?' cried Ruthie.

'–but a nice witch,' continued her father's letter. 'I told her I wanted something special for my special girl, and right away she said "a special girl needs a special bear!" Away she went and a few minutes later she came back with this one. I looked at it and thought he looks rather grumpy, and grubby, too. I didn't say it out loud of course, that would have been rude, but quick as a flash the old woman answered as if she'd heard me: "Ah well, as to the first that's not grumpy, that's his thinking face. Always thinking is Erasmus." "Erasmus?" I asked out loud. "That's his name," said the old woman. "And as to the second, to be sure, yes: he is on the grubby side. No doubt that's because of an adventure." "An adventure?" I asked, again out loud. "Of course!" she replied very seriously. "He's a magical bear, so he has adventures. You can't always be clean after adventures. But don't you be worrying about such things." Then I said to myself, but not to her, he's got no mouth. Again the old woman seemed to hear my thoughts, for she cried out, "He's got no mouth because he doesn't need one, seeing that he's magical." Well now,' the letter went on, 'after all that, how could I resist? I bought the bear and here he is. Which brings me to a very important question. You've heard of Paddington Bear, of course, and you remember that story I read to you about Christopher Robin and his bear… what was his name?'

'Winnie-the-Pooh!' cried Ruthie.

'Oh, yes, Winnie-the-Pooh,' the letter continued, 'and then there's Rupert and that American bear, Yoki... no, Yogi! Remember him? They were all very special bears when I was young. Well, obviously if the old woman is to be believed, this one is even more special. And magical! But the question for you now, my darling girl, is what's his name? The woman in the shop called him Erasmus, but I don't think he looks like an Erasmus, do you?'

Ruthie had no idea what or who an Erasmus should look like, but she shook her head anyway.

'Your father's right,' her uncle said. 'He's got to have a name.'

'Measly,' said Ruthie suddenly. 'That's his name.'

Uncle Ted looked puzzled, so Ruthie explained: 'He looks like he's got measles,' she said.

'Are you sure they're not little kisses?' her mother asked.

'That's silly!' Ruthie giggled. 'You can't call him Kissy,'

'But what do you know about measles?' asked her uncle.

'Measles is diseasles,' said Ruthie, 'They told us that at school.'

'I see,' said Uncle Ted, although he didn't really. 'Even so, that's not a very nice name.'

'I think it is,' said Ruthie, 'and so does he. He told me.'

'Did he indeed?' said Uncle Ted.

And so Measly it was. But there was still more to the letter, so Ruthie's mother read on: 'No doubt Mummy will say he needs a good washing, and she's right, of course.'

'Not in the washing machine! It will make him horribly dizzy,' Ruthie protested.

And then, almost as if her father had guessed what Ruthie would say, the letter continued: 'Handwash only, the witchy woman told me, and not to rub too hard or you'll rub away all the magic.'

Ruthie pressed the bear close to her nose and sniffed him loudly all over.

'Ruthie, don't do that,' said her mother.

'But he doesn't smell. Well, not bad.'

Her mother took the bear and gently sniffed the mottled material. There was a faint aroma of something she couldn't quite work out: first of herbs, perhaps like parsley and lavender, but then a second later of fruit like lemons, or was it pineapples? Well, whatever it was, it seemed a clean, sunshiny smell and not at all what she had expected.

'True, it doesn't smell bad,' she said. 'But we'll give it a wash all the same.'

'A very, very careful wash?' said Ruthie.

'A very, very careful wash,' her mother agreed. 'Even so, I don't want it in the bed.'

'What about on the bed? That's all right, isn't it?'

'I suppose so,' said her mother at last. 'But only on the cover, not inside. Is that clear?'

Ruthie nodded. Then she asked, 'Is that the end?' And Ruthie's mother picked up the letter again and read the last part:

'Anyway, my darling, I've got to go in a minute, but before I do, listen very carefully, for this is most important. You look after the bear and he will look after you and Mummy and keep you both safe till I come home again.'

As soon as her mother read those words aloud Ruthie forgot Measly in her arms and jumped out of the chair.

'When?' she cried.

'When what?' her mother asked.

'He's coming home!' she said. 'But when? When's he coming?'

For a moment her mother could say nothing. She read through the letter again quickly to herself. 'No, it doesn't... there's nothing...' she stumbled. 'No, he doesn't say.'

'Perhaps it's tomorrow, or even today!' cried Ruthie, and ran around the room swinging Measly high in the air. 'Daddy, Daddy, Daddy! My Daddy's coming home!'

But he didn't come home. Not that day, nor the next, nor the one after that.

*

Over the next few months life for Ruthie was not as bad as she had feared. The puff-puff bed was very comfortable, and with a much cleaner Measly held tightly in her arms – sometimes inside the bed – she slept better than she had for a long, long time.

Ruthie knew that Measly was special, perhaps even magical, as soon as she took him out of the box. And this was not just because he was a present from her father, but because... because.... Strangely, she could not say why the bear was so special, but that's just how it was, and from the very start she and Measly were the best of friends. He never went outside, he was too precious for that, but always stayed in the flat to protect it and Ruthie, and of course her mother and Uncle Ted.

Ruthie went to a new school and began to make new friends and to learn lots of new and interesting things. Even more interesting were the two new names she learned at Uncle Ted's. One was Eric, the other was Mrs Nosey.

Eric was Uncle Ted's hat. This was the woolly hat you read about earlier: a tall floppy hat with red and blue stripes, the sort to keep you very warm on cold, snowy days. Why was he called 'Eric'? A very good question, but no one knew the answer, not even Uncle Ted (which is just how it is sometimes with names). Anyway, he liked to wear Eric all the time, not only when he went off to his little studio down the road, but also around the flat, and all through the day and most of the night, too.

Because Uncle Ted was really rather bald, Ruthie had always supposed that he wore the hat to stop his head getting cold. Then one day in late September when it was quite warm outside the flat and inside, too, and they were about to have tea in the kitchen, Uncle Ted came back from his studio. As usual he was wearing the hat at the table, and as usual Ruthie's mother made him take it off and put it in his pocket. Although Ruthie had often wondered about her uncle's hat she had never asked him before. This time she did.

'Uncle Ted?'

'Yes?'

'Isn't your head very hot in that hat?'

Uncle Ted looked at her in surprise. 'You think I wear the hat to keep my head warm?'

'Yes,' said Ruthie.

'Oh, no no no no no!' cried her uncle. 'Eric stops the ideas escaping!'

'Eric?' said Ruthie.

'That's his name,' he said.

Ruthie was puzzled. 'Whose name?' she asked.

'The hat's, of course! Everything has a name. Doesn't it, Measly?' And without waiting for the bear to answer, Uncle Ted continued: 'You're all right, you see, because you've got lots of hair.' And then, as if to stop anyone else from hearing, he began whispering, 'but I haven't got much hair, so if I have an idea when I'm not wearing Eric it escapes–'

'Escapes?' Ruthie asked, also in a whisper.

'Yes! Escapes and flies all over the room and sometimes it's really difficult to catch it and put it back in my head and–' He stopped suddenly and gasped: 'Oh no, there goes one now!' And so saying he leapt up from the table and grabbed at the air near Ruthie's head. Then with his other hand he dragged Eric out of his pocket and in one quick motion thrust the escaped idea into the stripy hat and pulled it tight onto his head.

'Thank heavens for that!' he said.

'Oh, Ted,' said Ruthie's mother, with a sigh and a smile. And Ruthie laughed.

'You don't believe me?' said Uncle Ted. 'Right! Give me ten minutes and you'll see!' He reached down into the large canvas bag he always kept by his side, took out a pad of sketching paper and some pencils and chalks and began to draw.

Ruthie and Measly leaned over to see what he was

drawing, but quick as a flash Uncle Ted covered the paper with his hands and said, 'No peeking!'

'Come along, Ruthie,' said her mother. 'Why don't we go into the living room and perhaps,' she said, raising her voice, 'Uncle Ted will call us when he's ready.'

So that's what they did. Ten minutes later, almost exactly as Uncle Ted had promised, there was a shout from the kitchen.

'Ready!'

Ruthie dropped the book she'd been reading to Measly and ran back into the kitchen. There on the table was a drawing. It was a picture of a sandy beach by the sea. There were rocks, too, and standing by one of the rock pools was Ruthie. She was holding Measly up in the air and at the end of his foot, pinching it, was a large orange crab. And from Measly's mouth (which, as you know, wasn't really a mouth because he didn't have one), came a speech bubble, and written in that bubble were the words, 'Ow! Oooh! Ouch!'

Ruthie showed the picture to Measly and giggled. But then she said, 'But where's Mummy?'

'Good question!' said Uncle Ted, and he removed the first drawing to reveal a second one underneath. This second picture showed a rug on the sandy beach. Sitting on the rug, and surrounded by a picnic, was Ruthie's mother, and next to her laughing and holding up a jam and banana sandwich – Ruthie's favourite – was her father.

'Daddy!' cried Ruthie, and for a moment Measly

Ow!
Oooh!
Ouch!

was forgotten as she picked up the drawing and hugged it close. And although she was so happy to see her father there, Ruthie couldn't help but feel a little sad, too, and a tear came into her eye.

'There, there,' said her mother, comforting her. 'He'll be back.'

'When?' asked Ruthie.

And her mother ruffled her hair and said, 'One day, very soon.'

And Uncle Ted sighed loudly and pulled Eric off his bald head and said, 'I wish I had some hair to ruffle like that,' and they all laughed.

*

One day, after Ruthie and her mother had been living with Uncle Ted for a while, her mother met the woman from the flat on the other side of the corridor.

'She just stood there in the doorway, staring at me,' Ruthie's mother told Uncle Ted at supper that evening. 'Perhaps she thought I was a burglar.'

'That's Mrs Parker-Smythe. Keeps that window box of petunias you can see from the street.'

'Petunias?' said Ruthie.

'Flowers,' her uncle explained. 'Very pretty they are, too. She's won prizes for them. You'll often see her out on her balcony watering them, which of course gives her the perfect excuse to spy on everyone's comings and goings.'

'Oh, surely not,' said Ruthie's mother.

'Oh, surely yes,' said Uncle Ted. 'Always snooping, she is. If you want to know anything about anyone just ask her. A right nosey parker.'

'Mrs Nosey! Mrs Nosey! Mrs Nosey!' cried Ruthie and ran round the table.

'Sssshh, stop that!' said her mother, trying not to laugh. 'She might hear you!'

After that whenever they spoke about the woman in the flat opposite who always seemed to be watching them, they always called her Mrs Nosey.

Early one evening about a month later while the four of them – Uncle Ted, Ruthie, her mother, and Measly, of course – were sitting in the tiny kitchen having their supper, Ruthie's mother said:

'I went down in the lift with Mrs Parker-Smythe this morning.'

'Did you?' said Uncle Ted, as he buttered another piece of toast.

'I was on my way to the shops and she was taking newspapers to the recycling bin. I had quite a chat with her. She wanted to know all about me and Ruthie and why we're here.'

'Of course,' said Uncle Ted. He winked at Ruthie and whispered: 'She's…'

'Very nosey!' Ruthie whispered back.

'But the strangest thing,' her mother continued,

'was the way she held her handbag. Have you noticed that? She always seems to carry it with her, clutching it close as if there's something really valuable inside, like state secrets or her life savings.'

Up until this moment Ruthie hadn't taken much notice of the conversation, but she pricked up her ears when Uncle Ted replied: 'Oh, it's something much more precious than that.' Then he paused, leaned back in his chair, crossed his arms and waited to let his mysterious words have their effect.

'Well?' said her mother at last.

'Yes, tell us!' said Ruthie.

Uncle Ted leaned forward again, and said in a low, quiet voice: 'The eye.'

'What eye?' her mother asked.

'Her husband's eye. She keeps it in that handbag.'

'Uuuurggh!' said Ruthie, wrinkling her nose.

'Now, Ted, not at the table,' said her mother.

'But isn't it all squishy?' asked Ruthie.

Her uncle laughed. 'It's not a real eye.'

'I'm very glad to hear it,' said her mother.

'Oh,' said Ruthie, looking very disappointed.

'No,' said her uncle. 'It's made of glass.'

'Glass?' Ruthie had never heard of such a thing.

'Glass,' her uncle repeated. 'Sometimes when people lose an eye they can have a special one made of glass. And sometimes you can't tell the difference, unless of course you get really close.' And here her uncle closed one eye and stared wildly at Ruthie with the other.

'That's enough now,' said her mother.

But Ruthie wanted more. 'What happened to Mr Nosey's eye?' she asked. 'Did it fall out one day?'

'A good question,' said her uncle. 'I think it was an accident many, many years ago. Tell you what, next time we see Mrs Nosey we'll ask her.'

'You'll do no such thing,' said her mother. 'Now, Ruthie, drink your milk.'

Obediently Ruthie reached for her glass and drank her milk. But she was silent, and for a while she sat there with a puzzled frown on her face. Then she picked up Measly from the chair next to her where he was always seated during mealtimes, held him close to her ear and listened.

'Measly wants to know about the handbag,' she said at last.

'Ah,' said her uncle to the bear, 'I'm glad you were paying attention. Well, you see, when Mr Nosey died–'

'Ted,' said Ruthie's mother in a warning voice.

But Uncle Ted ignored her. 'When Mr Nosey died,' he repeated, 'Mrs Nosey pulled his glass eye out of its socket, plopped it in a little velvet pouch and there it sits to this very day.'

'Now, Ted, that's such a story,' said her mother.

'It's the very truth,' said her uncle. 'She told me so herself.'

'I don't believe you!' giggled Ruthie.

'Cross my heart and hope my teeth fall out,' said her uncle. 'A big green eye.'

'Green?' said Ruthie.

'It's certainly green now. She showed it to me. Never goes anywhere without it, And do you know why she keeps it?'

Ruthie shook her head.

'So Mr Nosey can keep an eye on her. In case she's very naughty.'

'Yes!' cried Ruthie. 'Naughty Mrs Nosey!'

'Now you two, that's quite enough,' said her mother. 'You shouldn't make fun of people like that.'

Clearly it wasn't enough for Uncle Ted, for suddenly he thrust his hand close to Ruthie's face in the shape of a large, sharp claw.

'That's not an eye,' Ruthie giggled.

'Noooooo,' said Uncle Ted in a deep husky voice. 'That's not an eye, but this is!' And so saying, he closed one eye and once again stared wildly out of the other until he looked more than ever like a startled owl. 'And together,' he continued, his voice falling even deeper, 'they're coming to get you!'

Still giggling, Ruthie screamed, jumped off her chair and ran out of the kitchen and into the living room.

'Now you two, we're having tea,' her mother called.

But it was too late. Already the hand and the claw had followed Ruthie into the living room, and when Ruthie escaped into the tiny hall where there was no escape the hand and claw followed her there, too.

By now Ruthie was screaming and giggling and laughing and screaming all at once as the face with the one staring eye made horrible gurgling noises and the hand that was like a claw drew closer and closer and–

But then to spoil their fun there came an urgent knocking on the front door and a sharp ringing on the tinny doorbell.

'What's happening? What's going on in there?' cried a voice in the corridor outside.

Uncle Ted opened the door a fraction to see Mrs Nosey standing on the mat.

'Is everything all right, Mr Bolton? I heard screaming.' And she peered into the flat as far as she could through the crack in the door.

'Oh, that,' said Uncle Ted. 'We were just having a little game.' He opened the door wider to show Ruthie. 'You've met my niece, haven't you?'

Mrs Nosey stared rather crossly at Ruthie. She didn't like little girls. In fact, she liked them even less than little boys. Little boys were always noisy and grubby. But that was only to be expected, so she could almost forgive them as long as they didn't come too close to her. Little girls, on the other hand… In her experience there was something sly and secretive about them, as though they knew something she didn't. Just like this little girl in the doorway, who seemed now to be fascinated by her handbag.

Then the little girl spoke: 'Are you going shopping?'

'Why?'

'Your handbag,' Ruthie giggled.

Mrs Parker-Smythe clutched the precious bag close to her chest. 'I... I...' she started to say, and then instead she asked, 'You're not keeping any pets, are you?'

'Pets?' said Uncle Ted.

'Pets!' Mrs Nosey repeated. 'Cats, dogs, that sort of thing. Strictly against the rules, you know.'

'Yes, of course, I do know. But why do you ask?'

'I've heard sounds. Animal sounds.'

'Oh, that's probably Ruthie talking to her bear.'

Mrs Nosey nearly fainted. 'B-b-bear,' she stammered. 'She's got a bear?'

'No, no, no. It's just a stuffed toy. Ruthie, show Mrs Nose– show Mrs Parker-Smythe your bear.'

Ruthie hesitated. She didn't want to share Measly with this strange old woman.

'Go on,' said Uncle Ted. Ruthie disappeared into the flat to collect Measly. 'They talk to each other a lot,' explained Uncle Ted. 'The bear was a present from her father.'

'Is that the father who's not here? The one who's gone away?' asked Mrs Nosey, with a loud sniff of disapproval.

Just then Ruthie reappeared with Measly and held him up to Mrs Nosey, who shrank back in fright, half expecting the rather strange-looking animal to attack her. For a moment she was open-mouthed and speechless, then finally she gasped, 'Well, it's most unfair of you to be so noisy.' And that was that.

*

The weeks and months continued to pass by, and suddenly it was almost time for Christmas. Those last few weeks were busy ones for Uncle Ted and Ruthie's mother, and for Ruthie, too, as school came to an end and the holidays began. As Christmas came closer and closer they bought presents for each other and for Measly, and lots of things to eat and drink for the days ahead. There was even a real tree – quite a large one which made the small living room even smaller.

By now Ruthie was fully settled in the flat and at school, and only occasionally did she think back to those happy days in the higgledy-piggledy house near the Heath which she had shared with Scruffy and her mother and her... Always when she began to remember too much and to feel sad she picked up Measly and had a jolly good talk with him, and then she didn't feel sad anymore.

Two nights before Christmas Eve Ruthie awoke from her sleep with a start. Measly was telling her

something, something urgent. Ruthie listened, then got out of bed, put on her dressing gown and slippers and went to wake her mother. After she had finished telling her mother, they both went to Uncle Ted, who was still awake and drawing in the kitchen.

'Ruthie says there's a problem with the gas,' said her mother.

Ruthie corrected her: 'Measly says.'

'Gas?' said her uncle. 'But we don't have gas. It's electric.'

'Uncle Ted's right,' said her mother, showing her the electric oven and hob.

'It's the same in every flat,' her uncle added.

'Measly said gas,' Ruthie insisted.

'And the boiler's electric, too,' said her mother, then asked, 'isn't it?'

'Has been for many years now,' her uncle replied. 'There's no gas in the building since they changed it all to electric in about 199–' Then he stopped suddenly, frowned, and said, 'Oh.'

'What is it?'

'There was a letter about six weeks ago. They started taking out all the old gas pipes in the basement, but then had to stop because they found asbestos.'

Ruthie had heard of asbestos. She didn't know what it was except that it was something very bad and unhealthy, and anyway– But this was no time for talking.

'Measly says danger,' she said firmly. 'Danger, we must go now. Everyone.'

Uncle Ted looked hard at Ruthie and saw that she was very serious. Then he turned to Ruthie's mother. 'If Ruthie says we're in danger and we've got to get out, that's good enough for me.'

'But Ted, she's just a child.'

'That's true,' said Ruthie, 'but Measly's not.'

That clinched it for Uncle Ted, but just to be absolutely certain he asked: 'One last time, are you sure about this? Really, really sure?'

Ruthie frowned, then looked at Measly. 'There's no time to waste,' she heard the bear say. Then she looked at her uncle and repeated Measly's message: 'There's no time to waste.' And her uncle believed her.

'Right,' he said. 'Most people have gone away for Christmas, but Mrs Nosey's still there. We'd better warn her first.'

While Uncle Ted put on some outdoor clothes, Ruthie's mother put on an overcoat and some sensible shoes and made Ruthie do the same, and then – together with Measly – they went out into the corridor and hammered on Mrs Nosey's door. There was no response.

'Perhaps she's gone away,' said Ruthie's mother.

'Not her,' said Uncle Ted. 'She's in there all right. Look, you keep knocking and I'll sound the fire alarm and warn anyone else who's here.' And as Ruthie and her mother tried to rouse Mrs Nosey, Uncle Ted

54

ran off down the corridor to the fire door near the lift and a few moments later an alarm sounded shrilly throughout the building.

Eventually from the other side of Mrs Nosey's door came a muttering and a grumbling, and then her thin voice asking: 'Who's there? What is it?'

'Quick, Mrs Nose–' Ruthie started to say before correcting herself.

'No time to explain,' said Ruthie's mother, 'but we need to evacuate the building.'

'Who says?' asked Mrs Nosey.

Through the closed door Ruthie's mother told Mrs Nosey that there was an emergency and that she needed to follow them down the stairs and out of the building as quickly as possible. Finally, there came the sound of a safety chain being undone, a bolt being drawn back and then one key turned and then another, and at last the door opened to reveal their neighbour in a fluffy pink dressing gown and hairnet.

At first she had a suspicious scowl on her face, but she looked at Ruthie and then at Ruthie's mother and something almost convinced her that they were serious. But still she said accusingly to Ruthie, 'If this is a false alarm, or a silly game, I shall be very cross. Very cross indeed.' And she went back into the flat to her bedroom.

'I assure you it's not,' called Ruthie's mother, and then to Ruthie she whispered, 'It isn't, is it?'

A few moments later Mrs Nosey emerged from the bedroom carrying a handbag. Ruthie recognised it immediately. After all, she had never seen Mrs Nosey without it.

'Oh, do be quick,' said Ruthie's mother.

'I'm hurrying as fast as I can!' Mrs Nosey said crossly. And resting the handbag on a small table in the hall she took down the old and rather shabby overcoat that she wore every day to the shops. Slowly she put it on, then dipping her hand into the pocket she took out a set of keys, stepped into the corridor, closed the front door and locked it, first with one key, then another, and then another.

'There's really no time for that,' said Ruthie's mother.

'There's always time for security,' said Mrs Nosey with a sniff.

The three of them set off down the corridor with Mrs Nosey complaining quietly at every step about her arthritis. When she got to the lift she pressed the button hard.

'No, no! Not the lift,' said Ruthie's mother. 'Too dangerous.'

'Well really!' said Mrs Nosey, and as they started down the stairs she moaned and grumbled about her old joints and how it really wasn't fair to treat an old woman so, especially in the middle of the night!

Halfway down the stairs between the fourth and the third floor Mrs Nosey stumbled. 'Not so fast!'

she cried. 'Oh, my poor feet. I think I need my other slippers.'

'No time for that. We must keep going.'

'But these are not very comfortable and I–' she stopped suddenly, then gasped: 'My handbag!'

'What?' said Ruthie's mother.

'My handbag! I left it by the front door when I was putting my coat on.'

'I'm sure it will be quite safe.'

'No, no! You don't understand. I can't go without it. I won't go without it.' And she took out her keys and began to climb the stairs.

'But this is an emergency!' said Ruthie's mother.

'My dear woman, I never go anywhere without my handbag. It has my... there's something very important, very special in there.'

Ruthie suddenly remembered what Uncle Ted had told her about Mrs Nosey's husband and the glass eye she kept in a velvet pouch. She tugged her mother's sleeve and pointed to her eye.

'Oh, I see,' said her mother. 'But surely you don't need it now.'

'I refuse to move a step further without my handbag.'

'I'll go!' cried Ruthie. 'I'm the fastest in my class!' And before her mother could stop her the little girl snatched the keys from Mrs Nosey's hand and in exchange thrust Measly into her arms and ran off up the stairs.

While Ruthie hurried upstairs to fetch Mrs Nosey's handbag, her mother and Mrs Nosey continued slowly down the stairs, sometimes meeting other residents as they made their way grumbling to the ground floor and out into the cold night air.

Someone must have called the fire brigade for a siren was heard coming louder and louder. Then a police siren was heard and an ambulance siren, too, and just as the fire engine, police car and ambulance all screeched to a halt in the square outside the block and it seemed as though the whole thing had been a false alarm there came a very loud bang from the basement, and a moment later a billowing puff of smoke and dust burst open the entrance doors. Then there was silence.

'Ruthie!' screamed Ruthie's mother. She started to run across the square and into the building, and Uncle Ted ran with her, but a fireman stopped them both and held them back.

'No, no, lady! Sir! You can't go in there!' he said.

'But my daughter–'

Uncle Ted was about to force his way through when a figure appeared in the doorway, coughing and spluttering and looking rather dirty. It was Ruthie. 'I did it! I did it!' she shouted, and held the handbag high in the air.

'Get that kid out of there!' yelled another fireman.

You'd think that Mrs Nosey would have been very

UNTAIN HOUSE

pleased when Ruthie presented the precious handbag to her, but no, not a bit of it. 'Pah!' she said crossly, snatching the bag from Ruthie's fingers. 'Was that your emergency? Well now, if you don't mind I'd like to go back to bed.'

But now it was Ruthie's turn to be alarmed. 'Where's Measly?' she said, tugging Mrs Nosey's sleeve.

Mrs Nosey ignored her and was about to take a step forwards across the square when there came a cracking noise from the block of flats, and a crack appeared by the doors Ruthie had just come out of. For a moment it was only a narrow crack but even as everyone stared the crack grew wider. The one crack became two and then three and then lots of cracks. They snaked their way up the front and then off to the left and to the right, and in no time at all the building was covered in them.

'Stay back! Everybody back!' cried the firemen and the policemen, pushing everyone away from the building.

Then with a deep rumbling and grumbling and creaking and groaning the building began to sway ever so slightly, uncertainly, as if it were not quite sure what to do next. And just when it seemed as if the block might topple to the left or to the right or to the front or to the back it gave a loud sigh and began to sink gracefully into the ground, one floor collapsing onto the floor beneath almost in slow motion, until finally the whole lot came to rest in a pile of rubble and a cloud of dust.

'Oooooh!' gasped all the people watching. All except Ruthie, who still tugged at Mrs Nosey's sleeve.

'What about Measly?' she said.

'What do you want, you silly girl?' said Mrs Nosey, even more crossly than before.

'Measly. My bear.'

Pointing to Ruthie's mother Mrs Nosey said: 'She's got it.'

'No,' said her mother. 'Ruthie gave it to you on the stairs.'

'Then it's still there!' said Mrs Nosey.

'No!' cried Ruthie. 'But you–'

But Mrs Nosey was in no mood for little girls. 'Never mind your stupid toy!' she complained. 'What about my petunias?'

'Oh, you and your–!' began Ruthie's mother angrily, then stopped herself from saying something very rude in front of her daughter. But Ruthie wouldn't have heard even if her mother had said something very rude. She was too upset, and bursting into sobs she fell into her mother's arms.

The rest of that night was a bit of a blur for everyone, especially Ruthie. She begged the firemen to let her search for Measly, but every time she got near to the ruined building she was moved away. At last a kindly old fireman promised to look very carefully the next day and to let her know if he found the bear.

Later that night or, rather, early in the morning for

it was now three o'clock, Uncle Ted, Ruthie's mother, Ruthie and their neighbours from Fountain House were moved to a nearby hotel where they were each given a small room to themselves.

As soon as she was up the next morning Ruthie begged to go back to the building to help the firemen and some other important people sift through the rubble for Measly. Of course she wasn't allowed anywhere near the area, but it comforted her to know that they were looking, searching, and that soon, any minute now, they would find her best friend.

But of Measly the bear there was no trace. No head, no paw, not a scrap of his body, not even a splodge of the lipstick red. For Ruthie it was too much. First her father had gone, then Scruffy, and now Measly.

Ruthie's mother tried all sorts of treats: her favourite chocolate cake, a new book, a new CD, a new DVD, a new bear or two or three, but nothing worked. Her happy smile which had once seemed as wide as a dinner plate was gone, and the sprinkling of freckles on her nose and cheeks had faded to a dull smudge. Even the thought of Christmas, now only a day away, held no delights for the little girl. And her mother worried that her daughter's tears would never end and she would never be happy again.

And then late on Christmas Eve, something very exciting happened. Outside the hotel in the street below Ruthie's window the lights were twinkling with brightly coloured decorations and the air was filled with the sound of carols and pop music and laughter as people hurried home with last chance Christmas shopping. Finally the street was quiet again, and so, too, was the hotel. Then just as a nearby church clock was striking midnight and the minutes were moving from Christmas Eve into Christmas Day there came the sound of voices in the hall. Half-awake still, Ruthie heard them but didn't really listen.

A few moments later there was a gentle tap at the door.

When the door opened this time it wasn't her mother, and it wasn't Uncle Ted either. Raising her head from the pillow, Ruthie wiped the sleep from her eyes and blinked. For a moment she thought the figure standing in the doorway must be Father Christmas. Or could it be...? And then she knew. She leapt out of bed.

'Daddy!'

He seemed shorter, and now he had a bushy red beard, but his eyes twinkled just as they used to, and as she ran into his arms and they lifted her up he felt stronger and more alive than she had ever known him.

Where Ruthie's father had been and what he had been doing, he never said. And perhaps he didn't need to, for sometimes there are just no answers, right or wrong.

And anyway, he was home and they were a family again, and in the end that's all that matters.

As for Measly... well, he's a special bear. So although the firemen found no trace of him in the rubble and ruins of Fountain House, not even a splodge of his lipstick red, it doesn't mean he isn't somewhere.

Does it?

Once Bitten, Twice...

The cat sat on the mat. Briefly. Then up she jerked and scratched vigorously behind her neck. Satisfied, she sat down again, but instantly sprang up to scratch and bite her tail. Almost satisfied again, she moved off the mat to the cool of the polished floor and attempted to rest there a moment.

Scarcely a second passed before she was up again. 'Aaaarrrghh!' she cried, scratching and biting several other parts. 'What is going on down there?' To her surprise, back came the answer:

'Just the usual!'

'I beg your pardon?' she said. 'Who are you? More to the point, what are you?'

'A flea,' replied a rather vulgar voice from one end of her fluffy young body.

'Me, too,' a similarly vulgar voice called from the other end.

'Ohhh!' wailed the cat. In her short, sheltered life she had never experienced such creatures. 'And are there more of you?'

'Nah, just the two.'

'Yeah, lucky for you!'

'I don't understand,' said the cat, scratching again. 'Why torment me so?'

'We're cat fleas, you ninny. What d'you expect us to do? Sing you a lullaby?'

Lifelong pals, the two fleas went everywhere together, and often worked as one. To emphasise their existence they now made the poor cat itch and scratch even more vigorously. Useless, of course. Paws and claws were no match for their attacks.

'Oooh, ow!' the cat gasped. 'But what are you doing here? This is a very private, expensive apartment.'

'Apartment? Oooh, lah-di-dah!' sneered the first flea.

Determined not to rise to the sneer the cat persisted: 'But how did you– I mean, who let you in?'

'You did.'

'Me?'

'Silly puss,' said the second flea. 'She's forgotten where she went this morning!'

'Of course I haven't forgotten!' she cried. 'I'm not stupid.'

'That's what you think.'

'I heard that!' she snapped. Of course she hadn't forgotten. How could she? Just a few hours earlier Daphne, her loving keeper and feeder, so proud of her new pet, so eager to show her off to their rich and titled neighbours, had taken her on a journey to the outside world. Leaving their exclusive flat on the 19th floor they'd travelled down in the lift, out through the smart lobby (with a special hello and stroke from the concierge), across the busy street and into the green, sunlit park beyond. And she on a bejewelled leather lead bought especially for the purpose! What an adventure that had been. And how they had both basked in their neighbours' admiration:

'What a pretty cat, my dear! You have such delightful taste', and 'Oh, she's adorable!'

Yes, the cat remembered with pride. What an adventure, or so it had seemed at the time. But now Daphne had gone off for lunch somewhere and left her to face the consequences alone.

'You can't expect to be outside in weather like this and not meet one of us,' said the first flea.

'Specially with such lovely fur,' said the second.

'Ow, stop that!' cried the cat. And then: 'How unkind of fate to inflict such an irritation! How cruel to–'

'Quit bellyaching!' said the second flea. 'If you was a cat of the world you'd take us as par for the course.'

'How dare you! I am not a cat of the world. I am–'

Here she broke off again to scratch and bite.

'Ooooh, stay still!' she cried.

The wretched creatures would not stay still. Instead, they jumped quickly to torment another part of the poor cat's body. (Aaarrgh, even as I write this I'm starting to itch!)

'Aaarrggh!' she cried again.

She ran back to the mat by the front door, and rolled on it over and over as roughly as she could, but the two fleas were too old and experienced to fall for such tactics.

'Haha!' they chorused. 'It'll take more than that to shift us.'

'I'll get you yet!' screamed the cat. Enraged by their disrespectful attitude, she tore off through the flat at a furious pace: through the living room, up the curtains, down the curtains, over the table and chairs and carpets and sofas, through the bedrooms, the bathrooms and every other space, till at last, almost blind with frenzy, she slid on the polished floor into the kitchen and swerved smack bang into her expensive china food bowl, which in turn smacked into the wall and broke in two.

'Ohhh!' she wailed breathlessly. 'Look what you've done! That was a present!'

'Not my fault,' said the flea at her head, somewhat dazed by the impact. He looked to his pal for support, but his pal's eyes were fixed on writing on a piece of the bowl. 'What's that word there? Er…mi… one.'

'That, you ignorant pest,' she said, 'is my name. Hermione.'

'Eh? What sort of a moniker's that?'

'Moniker?' Hermione asked, then added pompously: 'Explain, please. Unversed as I am in flea patois I do not know this word.'

'Name. He means "name".'

'Hermione's a very fine name,' she insisted with a dignified sniff. She didn't dare tell them that Daphne often called her "Princess".'

''Ermione,' said the first flea, pronouncing it in the most disdainful way. 'Sounds foreign to me.'

'Yeah, fancy foreign,' said the second. 'What you need, missy, is a good solid name like Bert here or Fred. That's me.'

'And don't forget Alf,' Bert suggested.

'Alf?' asked Hermione.

'My brother's name,' said Bert. 'Now there was a master. If 'e was 'ere you'd know it and no mistake. 'E could torment like no other.'

'One of the best, 'e was,' Fred agreed. 'Poor Alf.'

'Why poor?' asked Hermione. 'What's the matter with him?'

'Well, 'e's gone, 'asn't 'e? Not with us no more,' said Bert. And now it was his turn to sniff – or was it a sob? 'So, if you don't mind, we'll 'ave a moment's silence in memory of our dear departed–'

'A moment's silence! For a dead flea?' cried Hermione. 'This is ridiculous!'

'Ooooh, you're 'eartless, you are,' said Fred.

'I am not… whatever you say! And this has gone far enough. I demand you leave this apartment immediately.'

'Leave? Wish we could, missy, but we're stuck 'ere–'

'In this smelly flat,' said Bert.

'Now you mention it, what *is* that smell?' asked Fred.

'That,' said Hermione, 'is perfume.'

'Naff, more like.'

'Yeah, naff,' Bert agreed.

'Naff?' asked Hermione, puzzled again.

'Stink, poo, pong, 'orrible. In other words, "yuck".'

'Oh! But it's very expensive,' Hermione protested. She didn't care much for the perfume, or indeed for the smell of any of Daphne's lotions and potions, but she certainly wasn't going to admit that to these ruffians.

'But what do you mean, "stuck here"?' she asked.

'Simple. We need a cat to fix on, and seeing as 'ow we're on the 19th floor with no other in sight. Unless of course–'

'I see no other,' said Bert.

'In that case,' said Fred, 'you're it and we're stuck with you.'

'Don't think it's much fun for us either,' Bert complained. 'This place is far too posh.'

'You should have thought of that,' said Hermione, 'before you attached yourselves so rudely, so uninvited, to my… to my nether regions.'

''Ark at 'er! If you mean "bum" why don't you say so?'

'I am not that sort of feline. And this is not that sort of apartment. So please, get off my back and leave.'

'Sorry, missy. Can't do that, as I just explained. Unless, of course, you can get us outside again.'

'Outside?'

'On the ground.'

'And just how do you expect me to–?'

At that precise moment a shaft of sunlight pierced the half open window and pooled on the carpet.

'That's it!' she thought, 'I'm a cat. If I jump from a great height I'll land on my feet!' Having thought this thought she asked the two fleas: 'If I get you down to the ground again, do you promise to leave me in peace?'

'I promise,' said Bert.

'I promise,' said Fred.

'Promise on your mother's–'

'Now 'oo's being ridiculous!' said Fred.

'Very well,' said Hermione. 'Here goes.'

And scrunching up in the curious way that cats scrunch their bodies when preparing to pounce she propelled herself at the open window, sailed cleanly through the gap and into the hot, sunny air beyond.

'What are you doing?' cried Fred, clinging to her thick fur.

'Are you mad?' cried Bert.

'Not at all,' said Hermione, as she hurtled past the 17th floor. 'It doesn't matter how far we cats fall as we always land on our feet. Besides, I've got nine lives.'

''Oo told you that?' said Bert, as the cat gathered momentum.

'Well…' said Hermione, and then 'ummm…' as she tried to think where she'd heard such a fact. Could it be she'd got it wrong?

'No doubt that's true if you fall two or three floors,' Bert suggested, 'or even five or seven–'

'But 19!' said Fred. 'You're asking way too much there, missy.'

'Uh-oh,' thought Hermione, as the 10th floor went by in a blur, 'maybe this wasn't such a good idea.'

The two fleas, on the other hand, were having a wonderful time.

'Wheeeeee!' cried Fred.

'Double wheeeeeeeee!' cried Bert. 'What a way to go!'

They say that when you fall from a great height your whole life flashes before you. Hermione was still very new to life, barely out of kittenhood, so there wasn't much to flash. Even so, she knew enough to do what cats do, and just in time she did it. A few moments later her four legs hit the ground. Not the pavement but, as luck would have it, a soft flowerbed.

'Oooof!' she went as the air was jolted out of her.

The two fleas, of course, were fine.

'So long missy,' said Fred, hopping off. 'And thanks for the ride.'

'Yeah,' said Bert. 'See you around.'

'Not if I have any say in the matter,' Hermione groaned. The next moment a darkness closed her eyes.

A short time later her eyes fluttered open to find a big pink tongue licking her face.

'Ugh!' she squirmed, 'I'm being licked back to life by a slobbering dog. What an indignity!'

'There, there, Boris,' said the dog's owner, 'that's enough now.'

Boris had other ideas, but just at that moment Hermione's loving Daphne happened to return from her lunch. Seeing the gathering crowd she rushed over.

'Princess!' she squealed. 'What on earth–? and how did you–? Oh, get away with you,' she said, pushing the dog's owner out of the way. 'And take that vile animal with you!'

'Only trying to help,' said the man.

'If I were you,' said a bystander, 'I'd take the poor wee thing to a vet and have it checked it over.'

'Well, you're not me!' said the tearful Daphne.

Nevertheless, she did take Hermione to the vet's where – after a certain amount of listening to the cat's heart and lungs and gentle prodding and poking – she was pronounced as healthy as could be expected after such a fall.

'A bit of bruising here and there,' said the vet, 'so she might experience some discomfort for a day or two. She's young enough to recover, but that's definitely one of her lives gone. Oh, and by the way,' he added, as he handed Hermione back, 'I'd advise against taking her outside for a while. But if you do, make sure she wears a flea collar. Those little devils can be a real menace at this time of year.'

'Don't I know it!' said Hermione in a long, loud miaow.

As for going outside again? No, no! Once was quite enough. 'Besides,' she purred that evening, stretched out on Daphne's lap, 'it's so nice here. Warmth, comfort, delicious food and drink, far away from the wind and the rain and all those dreadful creatures.'

She shuddered at the memory.

'No. Here's where I am,' she purred even more loudly as she curled into a tight ball, 'and here's where I'm staying!'

And, as far as I know, she's still there.

About

Right now, people with a learning disability face inequalities in every area of life with almost 1 in 3 young people with a learning disability spending less than one hour outside their home on a typical Saturday.

They face barriers finding a job, accessing activities in their local community and receiving good quality healthcare. We tackle these issues head on by providing support in a way that meets individual needs and encourages greater independence.

We give expert advice and information that empowers people and their families. And we campaign relentlessly for changes that bring greater equality for people with a learning disability.

By supporting Mencap you will be helping us to support people with a learning disability to live the life they choose, and to do the things they love.

For more, please visit www.mencap.org.uk

John Foley

John Foley is an actor, puzzle setter and audiobook producer. After years of stage work he turned mainly to writing and audio. He has scripted and voiced hundreds of programmes for BBC English/World Service. Other audio work includes adapting numerous plays by writers such as Alan Bennett, Brecht, Ibsen, John Osborne, J B Priestley and Victoria Wood for World Service Drama and Radio 4, and producing for Macmillan, Naxos and Random House unabridged audiobooks of works by Boccaccio, Byron, Wilkie Collins, Dostoevsky, Hardy, Henry James, Kipling, Salman Rushdie, Trollope, Sir Walter Scott, Bram Stoker, H. G. Wells, Virginia Woolf and many others. Published work includes two volumes of 'simple and slightly silly stories', several reference books, a collection of musical anecdotes, stories for Disney comics and graded readers for children.

Alice Hawthorn

Alice Hawthorn is a London-based illustrator who specialises in portraying cats and dogs (alice@dogsdogscatsdogs.com). She uses a combination of pencil, colour pencils, watercolour, her beloved Rotring pens (which she came across while studying architecture many years ago) and Photoshop. Her Parson Russell Terrier, Cas, is a constant source of inspiration; with his strong opinions about things, he has a lot of input into her work!

Still available

direct from QuizzicalWorks
(visit: www.quizzicalworks.com | email: quizzicalworks@gmail.com)
or to order from Amazon and bookshops

Seven Simple and Slightly Silly Stories (Volumes I and II)

'Delightful and moving with a wonderfully sharp wit.'

Jim Broadbent

~

'I wish my kids were young again because I could hear them giggling in my head as I read each story.'

Melissa Canaday (Amazon post)

~

'Funny and thought provoking. Perfect to be read aloud and enjoyed by oldies and young'uns alike. A delightful stocking filler.'

Niamh Cusack

~

'Wonderful helpings of whimsy and truth in equal measure. I loved it.'

Julian Fellowes

~

'Every night for the past week I have been reading this extraordinary book and loved every story.'

Derek Fowlds

~

'Brilliant. I was so moved by the cockroach story. Like all good things I wanted more.'

Derek Griffiths

‘I so enjoyed this second volume of hyper-quirky children’s stories for grown-ups. Sometimes funny, sometimes sad, but always original and compelling.’

Francis Hallawell (Amazon post)

~

‘Stupendous, sumptuous and scintillating stories. I hope there’s seven or seventy more!’

Mathew Horne

~

‘A most absorbing delight from beginning to end. Always witty – but surprisingly sad, too.’

Celia Imrie

~

‘A delicious concoction – pithy, poignant and yes, seriously silly at times. The simple truths will make you smile, laugh and perhaps shed a tear or two.’

Pat Kies (Amazon post)

~

‘Absolutely brilliant. I will never cross a puddle again without sympathy. I love the stories. More please!’

Philip Lowrie

~

‘Stories which work at the level of fairytale, which are funny, wry, knowing and yet profound.’

Marion Nancarrow

'I dare anyone to read this and not smile! The title says it all really … utterly charming, totally unique, and yes, more than a little silly.'

Breakaway Reviewers (Amazon post)

~

'A delightful book ... full of silliness and joy, with a sprinkling of morality to boot.'

Maxine Peake

~

'Neither simple nor silly but wise and witty. A great read in a venerable tradition!'

Siân Phillips

~

'An enchanting collection … like the best Roald Dahl stories, gentle reflections on life and the quirks and foibles of us humans.'

Katie Scarfe (Amazon post)

~

'Wish I'd had this lovely book in my stocking as a youngster. Brilliant … I now want more please.'

Alison Steadman

~

'Really enjoyed the new stories – every bit as entertaining and original as the first collection.'

Juliet Stevenson

'I loved these stories. Slightly silly? Maybe, but wisdom and compassion lurks within these pages too!'

Ken Stott

~

'I'm reading John's gently beguiling stories to my children and we think they are fun and thought-provoking. Little gems like "The Mayfly" seem like an instant classic.'

Dominic West

Coming next!

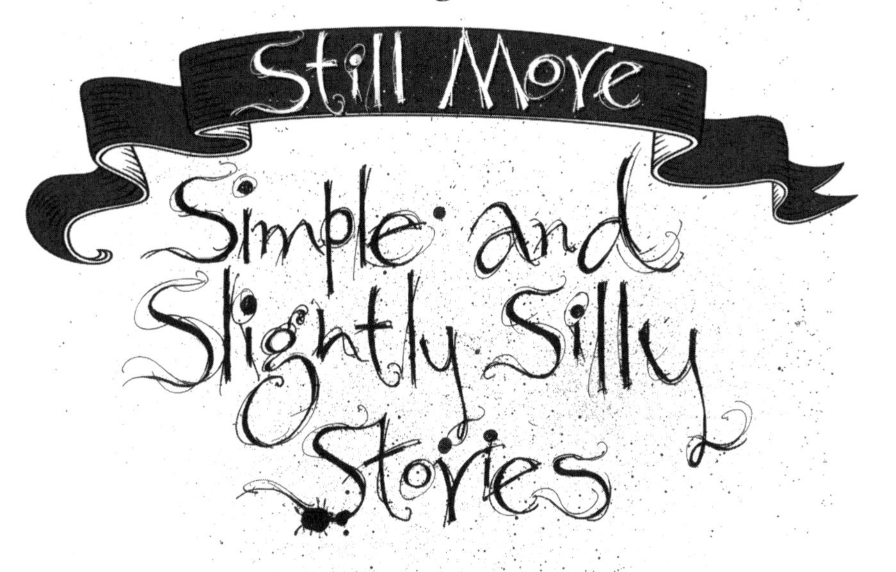

including **Hammer and Tongs**, **Christmas is Cancelled**, **The Nag of Shiraz**, **Spick and Span**, **The Lost Key**, and **The Shoemaker's Wife**:

Not so long ago and not so very far from here there lived in a village near the city a shoemaker. As shoemakers go he was probably one of the worst. He was lazy and incompetent, and the shoes he made were either too small or too large or, as most often happened, they simply fell to pieces. And though he knew his shortcomings (for he wasn't entirely stupid) he made no attempt to improve, and consequently he barely eked out a living. But somehow, and extraordinary though it sounds, he managed to snare a wife, and a beautiful and clever one at that. How that came about, and what happened both to her and to him is surely a story worth telling. So, if you're ready, here goes…